the amulet

THE TRAPPS FAMILY ADVENTURES

the amulet

By LAWRENCE E.R. ADAMS

Illustrations by ROBERT G. ADAMS

TRAPPS PUBLISHING

THE PUBLISHER:
Trapps Publishing
P.O. Box 212
Irricana, Alberta, Canada T0M 1B0

Library and Archives Canada Cataloguing in Publication

Adams, Lawrence E. R. (Lawrence Edward Roy), 1941-
The amulet / by Lawrence E.R. Adams ; illustrations by Robert G. Adams.
(The Trapps family adventures)
Includes index.
ISBN 978-0-9781532-1-2
1. Inuit--Canada--Fiction. 2. Inuit mythology--Fiction. I. Title.
II. Series: Adams,
Lawrence E. R. (Lawrence Edward Roy), 1941- Trapps family adventures.

PS8601.D454A65 2008   C813'.6   C2007-907520-7

Cover: Robert G. Adams
Printing: Friesens Corporation

DISCLAIMER

All the characters in this book are fictitious, any similarity between any living or deceased person is merely a coincidence.

For Christie, you are our Amy.

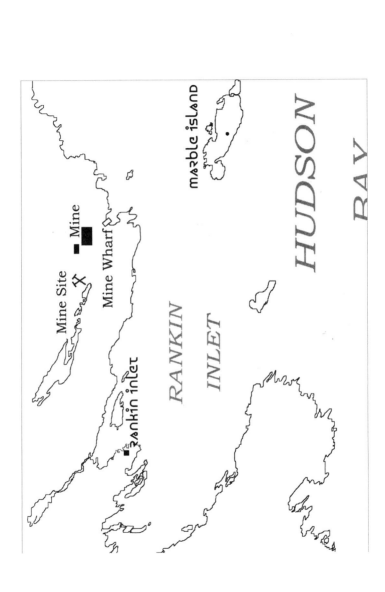

CONTENTS

PROLOGUE

It wasn't the call of the North that brought the Trapps family to the vast treeless region of Canada's North, known as the Tundra. This trip had nothing to do with the romance that "the call of the North" evoked; this wasn't even going to be a holiday. Numerous hours of backbreaking work would dominate the expedition, or so they thought.

Max Trapps, a world-class archaeologist, has led expeditions to numerous places in the world conducting excavations to uncover the secrets of the past. He has been chosen to conduct an archaeological dig at an ancient Inuit settlement. Workers at the Blue Diamond Mine, approximately thirty kilometres northeast of Rankin Inlet on the west shore of the Hudson Bay in the Northwest Territories, made the discovery while working near their airstrip. For the duration of the dig, the mining company is generously supplying the food and lodgings for the entire Trapps Family.

When Amy and her brothers, Ty and Parker, meet "THE OLD ONE," the secrets and mysteries of the North and the Inuit way of life will be laid bare before them. Nothing the kids might have done before they left their home in Calgary could have prepared them for the adventures they were about to experience. They were entering an environment that few people have ever seen and fewer will ever live in. It is a harsh and unforgiving land that holds untold beauty, mystery, and adventure for those who dare to accept its challenges. The North is home for the Inuit, the only race of humans who are able to live under its conditions without assistance from the outside world. The Inuit's ability to adapt to their environment allows them to reap the bounty of the North. Only the most adventurous and well-equipped explorers have been able to penetrate the Inuit's habitat and live to tell about it.

Amy's curiosity and her thirst for knowledge sometimes get her into jams that require the help of her brothers to get out of. She enjoys assisting her father during excavations and likes nothing better than discovering a relic from the past and unlocking its secrets. Ty is twelve, one year younger than Amy, and a gifted athlete. His favorite sport is hockey and if he were allowed, he would play it twenty-four hours a day. Parker, who is one year younger than Ty, doesn't possess his brother's athletic abilities, but his determination to succeed and to not be outdone by anyone makes him a worthy opponent. He possesses a photographic memory, which has proven to be an asset when his sister gets them involved in one of her many schemes.

After meeting the shaman Kadluk (the adults know him as THE OLD ONE) the kids now have the ability to communicate through their Inuas, a gift that is only bestowed upon shamans. An Inua is the spiritual occupant (spirit helper) that resides in all living and inanimate things.

chapter 1

what's that on your chest

Thursday, September 26, 1985

Dear Diary,
    The Old One told us about amulets, the powers they possess and what purpose they serve. It's hard to believe how crucial they are to the Inuit's way of life.
    Amy

Late Thursday afternoon the kids were riding skidoos and decided to ride out to the dig to see their dad and Bill Duncan. During the ride they practiced talking through their Inuas the way Kadluk, THE OLD ONE, had shown them.

About halfway to the dig Amy noticed a lone figure far off to her right. *"Who do you suppose that is over there?"* Amy cried as she pointed to the figure out on the tundra.

"With the clothes he's wearing, it looks like Kadluk; he's the only one I know who wears the traditional clothing - polar bear pants, caribou parka with seal skin mukluks," Parker exclaimed.

"Let's go see if it's Kadluk," Ty yelled as he turned his skidoo in the direction of the mystery figure.

As they drew closer to the lone figure, they could see that it was Kadluk.

"What are you doing out here?" Amy inquired as they approached Kadluk.

"I'm just coming back from hunting caribou," Kadluk replied.

"Why are you stopped here?" Ty asked as he looked suspiciously at Kadluk.

"I'm giving my dog team a rest," Kadluk told Ty.

"Jiminy-Willie-Peppers, where's your dog team? I can't see them." Parker cried as he looked around for the dogs.

"They're on the other side of that hill," Kadluk said pointing to a knoll behind him.

"What's that you've got sewn to your parka?" Amy demanded pointing to Kadluk's chest.

"They're amulets," Kadluk proudly announced.

"Why do you have them on your parka? What are they for?" Amy asked, peering intently at the amulets.

"Look at them closely and you'll see that one is a caribou and one is an Arctic fox. I carved the amulets in their images to flatter them. When I am hunting caribou or trapping foxes, they will know that I show them the proper respect and they will want me to harvest them. The animals do not make themselves available to the hunter who does not show the proper respect," Kadluk told the kids.

"Are the amulets only good for hunting animals?" Amy asked as she looked at the tiny amulets.

"Oh no, amulets are also used to protect us from evil spirits; they are our good luck charms," stated

15

Kadluk as he proudly stood before them showing off his talismans.

The kids peered in wonder at the intricate carvings, which had obviously been crafted with great care.

"Amy, have you found anything at the dig yet?" Kadluk wanted to know.

"Yes, some old timbers and bones, dad's really excited because he's sure they're from an old dwelling," Amy replied excitedly.

"Did you really carve your own amulets Kadluk?" Parker inquired as he stared intently at the amulets.

"Of course I did. For an amulet to have any power it must have been made by the person possessing it or must be given to an individual by the maker," Kadluk told the kids as he puffed his chest out with pride.

"Are those the only ones you've made Kadluk?" Parker blurted out excitedly.

"I have made amulets in the image of all the animals I hunt to show my respect for them, and I wear the amulet of the animal that I am hunting," Kadluk firmly stated.

"Can an amulet be made to represent more than one animal?" Amy asked as she looked intently at Kadluk.

"I have heard that an amulet exists that was made by the very first shaman; it was made in the image of all things. It has been lost for centuries but the one who finds it will be privy to its powers. It has been said that a jealous shaman stole it and that that shaman's group was banished from living near the shores. All Inuit live near water for it is necessary to sustain life. Yet the place where you dig is an old village and it is not near water. I wonder why that village was built where it is." Kadluk asked no one in particular, as if he was thinking out loud.

"Do you think that this is the village that you've heard about?" Amy shouted with glee as her curiosity grew.

"I don't know," Kadluk replied as he shrugged his shoulders and turned to leave.

"Where are you going Kadluk?" Parker asked not wanting the old shaman to leave.

"My dogs have rested enough, I'm going home," Kadluk said and started walking over the hill towards his dog team.

After Kadluk left, the kids drove side by side towards the dig site.

"Do you think Kadluk was trying to tell us something when he told us about the first shaman's amulet?" Amy inquired.

17

"No, I wouldn't put much stock in it, it's probably just an old tale. You know how things get exaggerated the older they get. Everyone adds something to the story and it gets blown all out of proportion," Ty replied.

"I don't know, everything he has told us so far has come true," Parker pointed out.

"Probably just a coincidence," Ty retorted.

"Well it would really be something if we found the first amulet and the village dad is excavating turned out to be the one Kadluk was talking about. Even if he doesn't seem to know if it's the village or not, it's still very unusual that it was built away from any shore," Amy said as they arrived at the tent that housed the dig.

chapter ii

the tent

The tent that covered the dig site wasn't just any tent. It had been used as a garage to store all the mine equipment before the permanent garage was erected this past summer. It was gigantic in size: 120 feet long, 50 feet wide, 30 feet high, and it resembled a huge cavern inside. Now that the permanent garage was complete, however, the tent had outlived its usefulness and was going to be destroyed. When the ruins had been discovered, Mr. Munro, the mine superintendent, decided to erect the tent over the ruins and use the remainder of the tent for storage. Without the tent, the dig could not have commenced and would have had to wait until next summer. Although it was cold inside, it still provided a safe haven from the elements.

The dig site was a favourite place for the kids, regardless of whether they were helping to excavate or playing. It was the equipment, the crates and the boxes of all sorts and descriptions that fascinated the kids the most. They spent hours rummaging through the equipment while playing all kinds of imaginary games.

Because it was used for storage, miners often came to the tent looking for equipment or spare parts that were needed to run the mine.

Some of the miners were friendly and some not so friendly. A few would stop and talk and show a genuine interest in the dig, but most didn't understand what they were digging for, nor did they care.

One of the favourite pastimes of the boys was to pretend they were driving the equipment that had been stored in the tent. This could consume a considerable amount of time and sometimes annoyed Amy. The time they spent skating and playing hockey she could understand; it was the other things that bothered her. She was usually preoccupied with the dig and couldn't see why they weren't as interested in it as she was.

"How come the boys always want to play with the equipment? Why don't they spend more time helping us?" Amy asked her dad.

"Well dear, boys, for some reason, like to drive equipment and the bigger the equipment, the better. Why, I don't know, I guess it's just because they're boys," Max replied.

"Well, I don't understand it." Amy sighed as she continued chipping away at the frozen ground.

"I'm just lucky I've got you to help me, dear," Max told Amy as he smiled at her.

"We wouldn't be here if Mr. Munro hadn't put this tent up, would we?" Amy said.

"No we wouldn't. We're just fortunate that Mr. Munro is the mine superintendent; not many people would have done what he has done for us," Max replied.

"The boys have played all day and haven't done a thing," Amy quipped.

"Life can't be all work Amy. The boys are still young and if they choose to play rather than help at the dig, that should be okay. After all, they do help whenever you need a hand or if they're asked," Max said.

"I know dad, it's just that sometimes I would like them to be more responsible," Amy replied.

Max chuckled to himself because Amy was forgetting the times that she too had whiled away the day playing with the boys as he and Bill were doing the excavating.

"It's time to go home - go find your brothers and we'll call it a day," Max said.

"Okay dad," Amy cried as she ran towards the south end of the tent to get her brothers.

Nadine was waiting for her family in the kitchen when they returned from the dig. Everyone was tired, some from working and some from playing. After supper everyone retired early.

chapter iii

what is it

Friday, September 27, 1985

Dear Diary,

   I couldn't believe my eyes when I brushed away the dirt and exposed the amulet.

   Amy

*   *   *

Amy heard someone in the living room and checked her alarm clock: it was 6:40 a.m., and she knew right away it was her father. There were many things to do at the dig and he wanted to get as much done as possible. Amy jumped out of bed; she would be going to the dig to help him and Bill.

"Morning dad," Amy chirped, as she entered the living room.

"Morning dear, did I wake you?" Max asked.

"No, I was awake, I thought it must be you. I wanted to go to the dig with you today and didn't want to miss my ride," she said, as she smiled at her father.

"Let's hurry, I told Bill I'd meet him at seven and I don't want to be late," Max informed Amy.

"I think the boys are going to come out after they do some work in the kitchen, but they'll probably have to skate for awhile. You know them and their skating," Amy sighed, with a laugh.

"Yes, that's very important to them. If they end up coming, we'll put them to work," Max said.

Amy, Max and Bill were soon at the dig and engrossed in their work. It was tedious work scraping and dusting away the debris from the layers of soil that had built up over the centuries. As Max had said, they had just scraped the surface and, indeed, this was so, for they had not progressed much beyond removing the topsoil. The permafrost presented a further problem: if they applied direct heat to it, it would melt. What would happen to the dig then? It would be anyone's guess. Would everything simply sink into oblivion? How far down was bedrock? It could be kilometers or meters, they didn't know. No, they would have to be patient and proceed layer by layer until the structure was completely revealed. They knew that in the time frame they had, they would never be able to completely excavate the site. They could only hope to do enough to warrant further expeditions to continue their work.

Amy was painstakingly chipping away the permafrost with a small chisel. Then, using a small paintbrush, she brushed the fine dirt to the side of the area she was working on. She had been working on this area for a few days and at first couldn't believe that she had uncovered something. She stared at the tip of a small object that had been revealed.

"I think I've got something here dad!" cried Amy as she stared at the object still buried in the ground.

"What is it dear?" Max shouted as he dropped what he was doing and rushed to Amy's side.

"Look at this!" she wailed as she pointed to the exposed object. "What do you think it is?"

27

Max peered at the object Amy was pointing at. He could see a small off-white coloured piece of the object that had been exposed from its icy grave. "I don't know, you'll have to uncover more of it and don't forget to document it in the register, dear," Max said, as he winked at his daughter. He didn't have to worry about the documentation; if he knew his daughter, even the longitude and the latitude of the find would be documented.

"What is it?" Bill inquired, as he approached Amy.

"I don't know but it looks very small and delicate, Mr. Duncan," cried Amy.

"Oh yes, and it looks like it's made of ivory too, that's a good find," Bill observed, as he peered at the object buried in the permafrost. "I've always said you were a good luck charm at our digs."

"Any ideas about what it could be, Bill?" Max asked his friend as they both stared at the exposed object.

"No, I have no idea what it could be, we'll have to see more of it," Bill replied. "You know before I came over here I felt tense and uptight and now I feel relaxed, as if I don't have a care in the world. I guess the walk over was just what I needed."

"It's odd that you should say that; I pretty much felt the same and now I feel a lot better. Maybe we've been working too hard and need some time off," Max said with a laugh.

"It's probably from kneeling so much and your back's getting sore," Amy said as she smiled at Max.

Amy was overwhelmed at her good fortune. She was the first to find an artifact that didn't appear to be part of the Inuit dwelling they were excavating! Her dad and Bill had been toiling for much longer than she had, and yet she had been the first to uncover a major find. Prior to this, the only thing that she had ever uncovered had been some partially rotten timber and bones. These were believed to have been part of the roof of the building.

"Well, we better get back to our sites, we've still got a lot to do. Do you want a hand here Amy?" Max asked Amy but he knew the answer before he asked the question. She had worked on a lot of sites and Max had complete confidence in her abilities to recover any object without assistance.

"No dad, I'm fine, I'll just keep working on it," Amy replied with a smile as Max and Bill returned to their duties.

Presently the three could hear the sound of a skidoo approaching, "I think the boys are here," cried Amy. "Wait until they see what I've found," she proudly exclaimed, as she ran to the door to greet her brothers.

Ty and Parker were soon inside the confines of the tent covering the dig.

"Come, look what I've found!" cried Amy, as she led her brothers to her find.

"What is it? What did you find?" queried Ty rather coldly as he followed his sister.

"Look!" Amy boasted, as she proudly pointed to the half buried object.

"What is it?" Parker wanted to know as he peered at the object buried in the permafrost.

"It looks to be very small, maybe it's an amulet like the ones Kadluk was wearing the other day," cried Amy her voice filled with emotion.

"Don't be silly, it's probably a child's toy," Ty whispered as he peered intently at the object.

"It might be an amulet, you don't know!" retorted Amy. Her brothers' lack of enthusiasm for the object was putting a damper on her excitement.

"Remember what Kadluk told us about amulets. He said you should make your own or be given it by the maker, otherwise it could bring bad luck," Parker reminded Amy and Ty.

30

"Leave it to you to remember that," Amy murmured with hurt in her voice as she looked at Parker.

"He's right Amy, Kadluk said that!" Ty stated as he stared at the object peeking out of the ground.

There is no greater fear than the fear of the unknown. The three looked apprehensively at the object. If it was an amulet, what powers did it have? Would the powers be released if they disturbed it? Would the powers have a positive or negative effect on them? These thoughts were going through their minds as they viewed the object. Doubt started to creep into Amy's head. If only Kadluk had not told us that amulets can contain good or bad spirits, these troubling thoughts that are formulating in my mind right now would not be there, she thought.

"Can you get it out, or should I help you?" Max asked, as he looked inquiringly at Amy.

These words snapped Amy back to reality; she didn't realize that she was just standing and staring at the object. What was it about this object that fascinated her? "No, I can dig it out dad," she said. The last thing she wanted was for someone else to dig out her find. Other than the timbers and the pieces of bone, this was the first significant find and she wanted to complete the task that she had started.

"Let us help you," both the boys chimed in, as they continued to stare at the object.

It was quite apparent this object fascinated the kids.

"Ty, take this brush, and when I loosen the dirt, brush it away from the object so we can see it better," Amy said handing Ty the brush as she started to dislodge the packed dirt. Amy patiently and cautiously chipped at the dirt, being careful not to touch the object with the chisel.

"I want to help, let me do something," Parker whined with a hurt feeling in his voice. He felt he was being left out of the recovery and wanted to take an active part.

"Here Parker, come over on this side and use this brush to sweep away the dirt," Amy said as she handed her little brother a different brush and patted him on the back.

Parker felt like part of the group again and took up his duties with enthusiasm. While Amy loosened the dirt, the two boys brushed it aside and before long the object was completely exposed. Being small, not much more than an inch long, it was easily extracted from its icy tomb.

The kids conversed thru their Inuas.

"Look closely, there appears to be two tiny holes on one side and a single hole on the other side of it. These

were probably the holes used to sew it to a parka, like Kadluk had when we saw him yesterday," Amy informed the boys with the thrill of discovery in her voice.

In the kids' excitement, the good and bad spirits that the amulet may harbor were quickly forgotten. They were holding something that may have been buried for centuries.

"I suppose you could be right. If it is a toy, it probably wouldn't have these holes in it," said Ty.

"Here, feel it, it's smooth and doesn't have a mark on it except for the holes, and yet when I look at it, it looks like there's an image carved in it," Amy said as she held it out to the boys.

"Let me see!" cried Parker taking the object from Amy.

The kids marveled at its smoothness, but at the same time, the intricate carvings were visible for all to see.

"This doesn't make sense, how can it be smooth and yet appear carved at the same time?" Ty asked with a frown on his forehead.

"I don't know, what do you suppose it represents?" cried Amy.

"It looks like an animal, maybe it's a polar bear!" said Ty.

"*Jiminy-Willie-Peppers! No, I think it looks like a fish or something swimming - maybe a whale,*" Parker said, as his eyes grew wide.

"*I think you're both wrong; to me it looks like something flying, maybe a bird of some kind,*" exclaimed Amy.

Max looked at the kids and noticed they were just standing there with funny expressions appearing on their faces. "Are you kids okay?" Max wanted to know.

"We're fine dad," Amy said with a smile on her face as she replied to Max.

"Well, don't forget to catalogue that item," Max reminded Amy.

"I won't dad," Amy said. "What does this look like to you? It appears to be many things at the same time; we all think it's something different."

Max peered at the object held out by Amy, "It doesn't look like anything to me, just a polished piece of ivory. What do you think Bill?" Max asked, as he looked at his friend.

"Well, that's a good question, let me see now. I'd have to say you're right - it doesn't look like anything but a small piece of ivory with three tiny holes in it. How do you suppose they made those tiny holes? I doubt they had anything like a drill when this thing was carved," Bill muttered, as he shook his head and stared at the object.

"Doesn't it look like there are carvings of animals on it?" Amy queried Max and Bill.

"No I can't see any carvings, it's just smooth," replied Max as he looked questioningly at Amy.

Bill just looked and shook his head from side to side indicating his answer – he couldn't see anything either.

The kids conversed through their Inuas.

"How come we see carvings on this object and yet dad and Bill can't see anything?" Amy asked her brothers.

"Maybe it's because we have shamanistic powers, like Kadluk said," Parker replied.

"That would explain it," Ty added.

"We'll have to take it home tonight and show mom," Amy said to Max. She'll be so happy that we've finally found something. It will really surprise her - I don't think she thought we would find anything so soon."

"Yes, I think you're probably right, she will be surprised. I think this calls for a celebration. What do you say we wrap things up and head for home?" Max asked.

Normally Nadine would be at the dig to share in the excitement of the find such as the one today. The uncovering would have created an air of excitement. Everyone would have shared the thrill of the hunt, and the drive to dig would have been so strong that nothing would have been able to pull them away. However, the excitement the kids displayed was contagious and their enthusiasm to share their find made Max and Bill change the daily routine. They would benefit from the shortened work day as well because they would get a fresh start in the morning. The discovery was like fuel, spurring them on in their quest to uncover the past.

"I'm for it - it won't hurt us to make a short day of it and it's almost quitting time anyway," replied Bill.

It wasn't long before the boys were heading home on the skidoos, while Amy, Max and Bill followed along in the van.

"Mom's going to be surprised to see us this early," Amy howled, "I can't wait to show her this object."

"Why don't we go to the kitchen and we can have her come over and join us. Maybe Gwen will want to come too?" Max said.

"That's a good idea, dad, when we get home I'll go get mom and Mrs. Munro, she'll like that," stated Amy.

Nadine heard the vehicles approaching the buildings and looking out, saw everyone pulling up in front of the kitchen. She knew something must be up so she grabbed her parka and was in the middle of putting on her gear on when Amy burst through the door.

"Come on mom, come to the kitchen, I've got something to show you. I'll get Mrs. Munro to come too," Amy shouted, as she turned and disappeared out the door.

Nadine was leaving her residence when Amy departed the Munro residence. Amy waited for her mom to catch up to her. "Mrs. Munro will be right over as soon as she gets her parka on. Oh! Wait till you see what I found mom!" exclaimed Amy.

"What is it dear?" Nadine asked her daughter as they walked towards the kitchen.

"It's an ivory object! Wait till you see the intricate designs on it, it's just beautiful! Wait till you see it!" gushed Amy.

When Amy and Nadine entered the kitchen, the men were already seated. Gwen, who hadn't wasted any time getting ready, followed them closely. Any excuse to get out of the house was a good excuse and this one appeared to hold more promise than some that she had used before.

"Seeing that everyone is here, I might as well call Bob to see if he can tear himself away from work and join us," Gwen laughed, as she approached the table.

"That's a good idea, give him a call. I'm sure he'll be interested in seeing this object also, knowing the way he likes to read up on local customs," Max said, as he looked at Gwen.

On the table in front of the little group lay the object in its plastic bag. Amy had already catalogued it and issued it a control number, as she had been taught to do by her father.

"Well, let me see your find," Nadine said, as she reached for the object. A sudden feeling of tranquility came over Nadine, which she quickly dismissed as the positive feelings she usually got when she had her family around her.

"What do you think it is mom? What does it remind you of?" asked Amy, looking inquisitively at her mother.

"It looks like a small piece of ivory with three small holes in it," Nadine replied, to her daughter.

"Do you see any figures carved in it?" Amy inquired.

"No, it's just a smooth piece of ivory. Why?" asked Nadine.

Just then Gwen returned from calling Bob on the radio, "He's on his way, he should be here in fifteen minutes," she advised the group as she took a seat at the table.

"Look at the object Mrs. Munro, what does it remind you of?" asked Amy, excitedly.

"Oh my, it's really small isn't it, what do you suppose it is? It doesn't really remind me of anything in particular; but you know looking at it I feel a sense of tranquility, like I'm very happy and at peace with the world. Isn't it funny I feel that way!" Gwen said.

"Now that you mention it, I had that feeling too and when I look at it I feel at peace - as if a weight has been lifted from my shoulders and I don't have a care in the world," Nadine sighed.

"That's funny you girls should mention that, for I had a feeling of relaxation when I first looked at the object," Max said.

"I did too! I was feeling kind of uptight when I first saw it, and then really relaxed afterwards," Bill added.

"Well, what do you think that means? You are all reminded of peace and tranquility by this object. We'll have to wait and see what Mr. Munro thinks it is and see if he agrees with you," Amy said, to the little group.

"Yeah we'll have to wait and see if Bob has the same feelings we have or if it reminds him of something else," Bill muttered, as he sipped his coffee.

"It's such a small object and it has no detail, and yet it gives us a sense of peace and security," Max said, as he viewed the little object. It's times like this that make a dig worthwhile. That is, when you can actually hold something in your hand that hasn't been seen for centuries. It allows you to wonder what the original owner of the object was like, how he lived, and what his life was like. Did he have a family? Did he have friends? Was he a leader of his people? The questions are endless. Of course, most of the answers will never be known as they are lost in time. All that remains is what he left behind and what we can interpret from his remains."

In time Bob Munro joined the group.

"Look, Mr. Munro, what does this object remind you of?" asked Amy, as she held it out to him.

"So this is what everyone quit work early for," Bob said as he took the object from Amy.

"Do you know what it is, Mr. Munro?" Parker excitedly blurted out.

"No, I can't say that I do, it just looks like a polished piece of ivory with three little holes in it.

I've never seen anything like it before. Does anyone know what it is?" asked Bob, as he sat down at the table.

"We were hoping you could shed some light on what it is. We've never seen anything like it either," Max said to Munro.

"No, I haven't got a clue what it could be. One thing I can say is maybe I should quit early every day. Sitting here I feel so relaxed I can't remember the last time I felt this good," Bob said as he peered at the object.

"Isn't it strange that everyone seems relaxed or as if they have a feeling of well-being when they look at the object?" Nadine said, looking around the table.

"The kids thought they could see carvings on it when they first found it," Max advised the adults.

"Oh, to have the imagination of a youngster again," Gwen said with a laugh.

The adults all nodded their heads with a knowing smile at Gwen's comment.

Amy spoke to the boys thru her Inua.

"We seem to be able to see things the adults cannot see. It may be best to say we feel as they do and not insist we can see the carvings as they may not understand," Amy told her brothers.

41

"Yes, that's very interesting, it's almost like the object has a mind of its own and it's trying to tell us something," Max muttered.

"Oh, you don't believe that," Nadine scoffed while looking at her husband. "You're not superstitious!"

"No, I'm not superstitious. Usually there's a scientific explanation for everything; however, there are people who believe in the supernatural. There are a number of things that science has no explanation for. Sometimes it makes one wonder just what is going on in the universe when there's no logical explanation for things that occur."

With the excitement of the find over for the adults, they made small talk while drinking their coffee. They did not pay any attention to the kids and, as a result, they completely missed the expressions that came and went on the kids' faces as they conversed thru their Inuas.

chapter iv

the amulet

"Kadluk said the first shaman carved an amulet in the image of all things, remember? When we look at this object we see carvings of different things and the adults just have a feeling of peace and serenity. Do you think it could be the first amulet?" Amy wanted to know.

"Don't be silly, we don't even know if that story is true," Ty replied.

"I don't know," Parker said. *"A lot of strange things seem to be happening and we don't have an explanation for them."*

"We'll have to ask Kadluk the next time we see him," cried Amy.

"Yeah, I'd like to hear what he has to say about this. Like I said before, it's probably a toy and not an amulet at all," Ty scoffed.

"We'll see, little brother!" Amy replied.

"Why don't you ask the object's Inua? You have the ability to speak to it," Parker said to Amy.

"You're right, I never thought of that. You and your mind! You think of everything," Amy said to Parker.

The kids just stared at the object.

"You know when you turn it, you see something different. Have you noticed that?" Ty asked as he rotated the amulet in his hand.

"Yes, I see different things as you turn it, what do you think that means?" Amy inquired.

"Are you going to talk to its Inua Amy?" cried Parker rather impatiently.

"I don't know what to say," Amy replied and shrugged her shoulders.

"Just ask it if it's the first amulet that was made by the first shaman," said Parker.

"Are you the first amulet that was made by the first shaman?" Amy asked the amulet.

"Yes I am," came the reply.

The kids were beside themselves with glee and awestruck at the same time. They had found something that had been buried for centuries and now they had been instrumental in bringing it to life.

"What should I ask it now?" wailed Amy as she looked at her brothers.

"Kadluk said its powers would be conferred upon the finder; ask if this is so." Parker said to Amy.

"Are the powers you possess conferred to your finder? Amy asked.

"Yes," came the reply.

"What are your powers?" cried Amy as the excitement grew in her voice.

"I possess the power to protect the one who bears me," the amulet's Inua replied.

"How do you do that?" asked Amy with an inquisitive look on her face.

"I was made in the image of all things; when someone bears me, anything that looks at the bearer, sees himself. No one ever does anything to hurt themselves

and therefore, they will not harm whoever bears me," came the reply.

"Do you mean that no animal, no matter how vicious it is, will harm me while I'm wearing you?" Amy queried.

"That is correct, no harm will come to you," replied the amulets Inua.

"Why is it that when we look at you we see carvings of animals and different things yet the adults can't see them?" inquired Parker.

"It is because you have the abilities of a shaman; only a shaman can see my carvings. Others who look at me only see their inner self and are left with a sense of peace and tranquility. That is why the person who bears me is protected," replied the Inua.

"Kadluk said that you were stolen from the first shaman, your maker. Is that true?" questioned Ty with doubt in his voice and a frown on his forehead.

"That is correct, but that happened long ago and the transgressor placed a heavy burden on his people for his sins. They suffered greatly and were banished from the shores for as long as they lived," the Inua informed the kids.

"That is why this village is here, so far from the shore. This is the village of the wrongdoer, isn't it?" Amy shouted excitedly.

"Yes it is," replied the Inua.

47

"Did the first shaman ever get you back? Did he ever find you?" asked Ty with concern in his voice.

"No, I was brought to this place and buried by the wrongdoer after he stole me. Before he could retrieve me, he met his fate and was never seen again. His people were banished to this spot for his sins and they endured a miserable existence until they finally perished," said the Inua.

"Jiminy-Willie-Peppers! What happened to them?" howled Parker.

"Because they were not close to the ocean, they didn't have access to the seals that are necessary to sustain life during the long winters. There is no ready access to fresh water from here, so during the summer they had to travel far distances to obtain it. This location is not near any of the normal migration routes of the caribou and few, if any, ever pass this way. After the wrongdoer perished, the people did not have a shaman to turn to during their times of difficulty. With no one to turn to and no one to guide them, they slowly perished. Some went to hunt or fish and never returned, so their families starved because they had no food. Some saw the utter despair, how futile it was to continue, and they just gave up and slowly died away," said the Inua.

"How sad it is to have to suffer for the wrongdoing of others, especially when they're supposed to be helping you. To think it was all caused by the

jealously of their shaman," lamented Amy. There was genuine sorrow in her voice, just thinking of the hardships The People must have suffered because of their shaman's actions.

"Wait until Kadluk hears that we have found the first amulet!" exclaimed Parker.

"Who is Kadluk?" asked the Inua.

"Kadluk is our friend; he is an Inuit shaman and he is teaching us to be shamans," said Amy.

"You are lucky to have such a friend," said the Inua.

"Yes, we are. He has shown us what is expected of a shaman and what powers a shaman possesses. Everyone else calls him THE OLD ONE, but we know him as Kadluk," said Amy rather proudly.

"THE OLD ONE, yes, I have heard of him," replied the Inua.

"How did you hear about THE OLD ONE?" Amy wanted to know with a surprised look on her face.

"I've heard his name mentioned many times," replied the Inua.

"By whom?" queried Ty?

"I may have been buried in this icy grave for many changes of season, but I have still been able to hear the other Inuas talk and tell of the great feats of The People as they walk through life. THE OLD ONE'S name

49

has been sung in praise at many feast gatherings. He is held in high regard by THE PEOPLE." The kids listened intently with renewed respect for Kadluk.

"How old is THE OLD ONE?" Ty blurted out as he stared at the amulet.

"It matters not! How old is anything? Life is not counted by age, but by deeds. To have one's name sung in praise at a feast gathering is more important than the time it took to accomplish the feat that one is being praised for," the Inua said sternly.

"He's even shown us how to fly," Parker shouted excitedly.

"Has he? That is good, flying is one of the most important powers a shaman should possess," observed the Inua.

"He even told us about you," Ty said to the Inua.

"How did he know about me?" asked the Inua.

"He said that the first shaman had made the first amulet in the image of all things and that you had been stolen by a jealous shaman and you had not been seen since. Although the first shaman searched for you, he never succeeded in finding you. He said it was a story handed down through the ages, but he didn't know if it was true or not as it had happened so long ago," remarked Amy as she peered at the amulet.

"Now we have found you, so we know the story to

be true," cried Parker with excitement bubbling in his voice.

"I just know Kadluk will be pleased when we tell him about you. I can't wait to see the expression on his face!" howled Amy.

"Boy, he's going to be surprised," Ty quipped as he looked at the amulet and shook his head. He knew things he thought were impossible were now happening, but he was having trouble accepting them at face value.

*   *   *

"Come on, kids, it's time to go home," Max called out, as he got up from the table.

The adults spent the afternoon talking about the dig and what further treasures they may uncover. What secrets did the earth hold and would the earth give them up? Only time could answer these questions. Their spirits had been buoyed considerably with the discovery of the little amulet that now graced the table in front of them. The afternoon wore on and after the group had eaten, it was time to retire. All were in good spirits when they left the kitchen to return home.

Little did the adults know that the dig had already yielded a treasure valuable beyond their wildest imaginations. Would the adults ever be privy to the knowledge the kids now shared? How might the treasure affect them in the future?

Max made Amy responsible for the safe keeping of the little amulet and wouldn't let it stray far from her hand. When she returned home she put it on her dresser so that she would not lose it. Amy went to the boys' room before going to bed.

"Do you think we should tell mom and dad about the amulet?" Ty wanted to know.

"No, it's obvious they do not possess the traits of a shaman because they cannot see the carvings on the amulet. I don't think they would understand if we told them. It is better to just keep it to ourselves until we talk to Kadluk," Amy advised her brother.

"Amy's right, they wouldn't understand; only Kadluk will understand," Parker added.

Ty nodded his head in agreement.

"Okay then, I'll see you in the morning," Amy said as she left the boys' room.

Chapter V

Life's a mystery

With breakfast over, the kids decided to stay in the kitchen and help the cooks clean up and get ready for the next meal. When they were finished and were getting set to leave, Kadluk walked through the door. He immediately went to his chair and the Inuit ladies began fussing over him.

The kids conversed with Kadluk thru their Inuas.

"We've got some questions for you and I want to tell you about the amulet we found," Amy said to Kadluk.

"We found the first amulet that was made by the first shaman," Parker blurted out in his enthusiasm.

"Did you really! What makes you think it is the first amulet?" Kadluk queried as he began putting spoonfuls of sugar into his piping hot tea.

"Amy talked to its Inua and it said it is the first amulet and it had been stolen just as you said," Parker quickly told Kadluk.

"Oh I see!" said Kadluk. *"I would like to see this amulet, where is it?"*

"I have it in my room!" Amy cried with pride in her voice.

"When I have finished my tea, you must show me this amulet," Kadluk said.

"Are you coming to our house?" asked Amy.

"No, when I am ready to leave you can bring it over and I will look at it outside the kitchen. No one knows we can converse and they would not understand if they did know. To try to explain shamanism to some people is an impossible undertaking, for some will never understand," Kadluk replied.

"Do you think it is the first amulet Kadluk?" Parker asked with concern in his voice.

"I do not know, only time will answer that question," Kadluk said as he continued to eat cookies and drink his tea.

The kids ate cookies and waited what seemed to be an eternity before Kadluk finally had his fill. When his hunger was satisfied the kids could see that he was getting ready to leave.

"You can fetch the amulet now and I will meet you outside," Kadluk informed the kids as he was walking towards the door.

In a flash the kids were up and running for home to get the amulet.

"Do you think it's a good idea to take the amulet to him? It seems funny that he wants to see it outside the kitchen" remarked Ty with concern in his voice.

"What do you mean?" cried Amy with an annoyed look on her face.

"I just think it's funny that he doesn't want to come to our house or see it in the kitchen. Why do we have to take it outside?" queried Ty.

"Do you think he's going to steal it from us?" shouted Amy showing concern.

"Kadluk wouldn't do that," Parker stated flatly.

"How do you know? You don't know anything about him!" retorted Ty rather huffily.

"Well after all he's shown us I don't think he would do anything like that!" shot back Parker looking at his brother.

"I think Parker's right, and besides, he had a logical explanation for asking us to bring it to him," Amy said to Ty.

"What logical explanation would that be?" Ty quipped rather dryly.

"He said no one knows we can converse and no one would understand if they did know. Now if he came to our house or if we took it to him in the kitchen, people would know that we can communicate - how else would he know we have the amulet?" Amy retorted rather bluntly.

"Yeah, I guess you're right, but you better be on guard. If anything happened to that amulet, you'd have a tough time explaining it to dad," Ty warned, again showing concern.

"I'll be careful and, besides, you'll be there so if anything happens, you'll be explaining to dad also - so I won't be the only one," gloated Amy looking at Ty with a smug smile on her face.

"Hurry up you two and quit arguing. Kadluk isn't going to wait all day for us," Parker reminded his siblings.

When they returned they could see Kadluk off to the east of the kitchen near his Komatik. His dogs lay in the snow where he had staked them upon his arrival.

"Here it is Kadluk," Amy called as they approached him.

She held out the amulet but Kadluk only looked at it. He didn't reach for it.

"Here, take it, see if it is the first amulet," Amy said as she held the amulet out to Kadluk. As she observed him, she thought she detected a look of recognition in his eyes, but it was only a flash and then it was gone. *"Do you recognize this amulet? Have you seen it before?"* Amy wanted to know.

Kadluk took a quick step back as if he was recoiling from the amulet. *"It matters not. I can see it from here - turn it in your hand so that I may see its carvings,"* Kadluk replied sternly, keeping his distance.

"What's the matter? Don't you want to hold it?" wailed Amy as she rolled the amulet over in her hand.

"No," replied Kadluk as he cautiously peered at the amulet.

"Why don't you want to hold it, Kadluk?" asked Ty with concern in his voice.

58

"*An amulet only has powers for the person who carved it or for the person the carver gives it to. After an amulet has been used, some lose their powers and are inhabited by a Tarrak. You must always be on your guard against a Tarrak for they will do you harm,*" warned Kadluk.

"*What is a Tarrak?*" asked Amy.

"*When relatives of a dead person do not adhere to certain customs, its soul becomes enraged and malicious. This dark angry spirit is known as a Personal Shade or Tarrak,*" said Kadluk.

"*Jiminy-Willie-Peppers, is that why you won't touch the amulet?*" howled Parker with concern in his voice.

"*That is correct. I can see it has been carved in the image of all things, for I have never seen an amulet that can show so many carvings at the same time. However, when you talked to the amulet's Inua, you may have been talking to a Tarrak trying to trick you. One has to be forever on his guard against a Tarrak because it will use any guise to wreak havoc and harm you,*" Kadluk said, staring at the amulet.

"*This is just great! What kind of a mess have we got ourselves into? What are going to do now?*" cried Ty with real concern in his voice as he looked at Amy and then Parker.

"Jiminy-Willie-Peppers, you'll help us, won't you Kadluk?" Parker pleaded as he looked at Kadluk.

The kids could think of only one thing: Kadluk's reaction when Amy held the amulet out to him. They vividly remembered the way he stepped back and wouldn't touch the amulet. If Kadluk was afraid of Tarraks then they, too, had better be afraid of them, whatever they were. The elation the kids felt when they thought the amulet could only bring them good luck quickly faded when they realized they actually didn't know anything about it and it could be hiding dark and foreboding secrets. The sinking feeling they were experiencing in their stomachs just wouldn't go away.

chapter vi

the test

Amy was the first to regain her composure and with a shaky voice asked, *"how can we tell if it's a Tarrak or the amulet's Inua, Kadluk?"*

"We have to test it. If the powers have left the amulet and it is inhabited by a Tarrak, it will not be able to protect you as it said it could. In its blind rage, the Tarrak only wants to get revenge and will use any method to accomplish that end. That is why one should never take an amulet unless it is given to you by the maker," Kadluk warned the kids.

"How do we test it?" pleaded Amy, her voice still shaky.

"We can test it using my dogs. No one dares walk near working dogs because they will tear you to pieces. They can't even stand each other, which is why I have to stake them apart when they're not working. If I didn't, they would kill each other," Kadluk informed the kids.

"How do we test it against your dogs?" Amy cried as she stared at Kadluk.

"If the amulet has the powers the Inua says it has, the dogs will not harm you when you walk among them," said Kadluk.

"Isn't that kind of risky?" howled Ty with concern in his voice.

"Yes, it is, but that is the only way we can test its powers right now. There isn't anything else here that presents any danger to you!" Kadluk said with authority, as he looked around.

"That's right, there's nothing dangerous here except the dogs," Parker muttered with eyes as wide as saucers as he looked from side to side.

The nearest dog was some thirty yards from where the kids were conversing with Kadluk. Like most working dogs that weren't working or eating, Kadluks' dogs were lying on their bellies with their heads resting on their hind legs and their tails curled over their heads for protection from the elements. Right now they were in this position and not paying attention to the group because they were too far away to offer any danger to them. This was about to change.

"I-I don't know - I haven't heard anything good about walking into a bunch of working dogs. I'm not sure I want to do that," Amy hesitated.

"Give the amulet to Ty and come with me. I can protect you from my dogs and we should find out if this is the first amulet and if it has the power to protect you as the amulet's Inua said!" Kadluk ordered Amy as he turned and started walking towards the nearest dog.

"Jiminy-Willie-Peppers, I don't like the looks of this!" Parker quipped as the dog Kadluk was heading for jumped to its feet and tried to stretch its lead as far as he could.

The dog backed away from Kadluk and when it reached the end of its lead it was like a wild caged animal, with bared fangs and snarling and taking vicious bites out of the air. Anything or anyone who came within reach of this animal was going to have eighty pounds of fighting fury and razor sharp fangs to contend with.

"I will walk down the lead," Kadluk advised the kids.

"What is a lead?" cried Amy.

"The lead is the cord that attaches the dog's harness to the Komatik. Some leads today are made of rope but I still use the old ways and mine are made of strips of

braided sealskin. They can be any length you want them to be," Kadluk said as he looked at Amy.

"Oh I see," replied Amy.

Kadluk walked down the lead making sure his feet never left it. With the dog straining to get away from his approaching enemy, the lead remained taut. When he was about three feet from the animal, Kadluk stopped. The dog didn't quit his struggling and was just going crazy pulling backwards trying to get away.

"Walk up beside me and a little to the left and see what the dog does," Kadluk directed Amy.

As soon as Amy drew even with Kadluk the dog lunged at her.

"Look out!" Ty yelled.

Parker was standing back watching the events unfold before him and his eyes were getting as big as saucers as the danger grew.

With a gasp for air Amy jumped back and out of reach of the dog.

"Go get the amulet from Ty and come back here!" Kadluk commanded.

"I don't know if I want to, that dog scares me," Amy muttered as her voice clearly showed that she had been shaken by the experience.

"Get the amulet, we must see if it has any powers!" Kadluk demanded.

65

Amy retraced her steps to Ty and retrieved the amulet.

"Are you sure you want to do this? That dog is going crazy, he'll tear your arm off if he gets hold of you!" Ty howled.

"I-I don't have any choice, we've got to know," Amy stuttered.

"Then let me do it," Ty pleaded.

"No I'm the oldest, if anything happens it'll be my fault," Amy uttered trying to muster as much courage as she could.

"Well, be careful, I don't like this," Ty warned with concern in his voice.

Amy turned and slowly walked towards Kadluk who was standing on the lead. Her steps slowed considerably the closer she got to Kadluk. She didn't like the reception she received from the dog the last time she approached and was not looking forward to a repeat of the same.

"Come on, Amy, I can't stand here all day," Kadluk gently chided.

"I-I'm coming," Amy muttered.

"Come up on my left again, be careful and go slow," Kadluk said, motioning with his left arm,

As Amy approached from Kadluks' left, the dog continued its struggle to get away but never

66

lunged at her, it never even acknowledged that she was there.

"Go closer to the dog," Kadluk urged never taking his eyes off the dog.

Carefully Amy inched closer to the dog. It never even looked at her it just concentrated on Kadluk and continued its struggle.

"The dog is not paying any attention to me, what does that mean?" Amy sighed with relief in her voice.

"It means you are being protected, the amulet has powers!" said Kadluk with a grunt of satisfaction.

Amy walked closer to the dog and was completely ignored.

"Walk over to that dog," Kadluk pointed to a dog twenty feet away who was watching the goings on with interest but who didn't feel threatened because of the distance between them.

As Amy approached the dog it ignored her and was concentrating on Kadluk and the dog that was going wild trying to get free.

"It acts like I'm not even here," Amy yelled, the joy in her voice could clearly be heard.

"Take the amulet back to Ty and let him try it," Kadluk said to Amy.

With the amulet in his hand Ty apprehensively approached Kadluk and the dog. He got the same response Amy had received from the dog, he was completely ignored.

"It works for me!" Ty excitedly shouted.

"Yes, it appears to. Now give it to Parker and see if it works for him also," Kadluk said.

Parker approached Kadluk with his eyes wide open and his breath coming in short gasps. The dog snarling and gnashing its teeth didn't give him any comfort.

As he passed Kadluk and approached the dog, he was relieved to see that it also ignored him.

"I-I did it, the dog likes me!" Parker sighed with relief.

"Don't think for a minute that dog likes you: you are being protected by the amulet - that dog would just as soon tear you apart as look at you," Kadluk informed Parker.

"It works! It protects us just like the amulet's Inua said it would," cried Amy.

"Yes, so it would seem, but why does it protect all of you when it is only one amulet and an amulet only protects one person?" mused Kadluk.

"Talk to the amulet's Inua Kadluk - it will tell you why," Parker shouted out in his excitement.

"Yes, here Kadluk, talk to the Inua," Amy said holding the amulet for Kadluk to take.

68

Kadluk stood back from Amy for he knew the powers of an amulet and this was not his amulet and was therefore forbidden to him. He studied the amulet held out to him before he spoke.

"How are you able to protect three when an amulet is made for only one person?" Kadluk asked the amulets Inua.

"The first shaman, my creator decreed that whoever found me would be privy to my powers and as these three found me, my powers will be conferred to them," replied the amulets Inua.

"But how can that be?" queried Kadluk.

"I have the ability to replicate myself to conform with my creator's wishes. These three found me and therefore I will replicate myself to offer them my protection and to fulfill my creator's wishes," said the amulets Inua.

"It is true, then. Just as it was spoken by the old ones, this is the first amulet that was made by the first shaman, and from now on, you will have protection a mortal man can only dream of," Kadluk advised the kids.

CHAPTER VII

it boggles the mind

"*Jiminy-Willie-Peppers!*" exclaimed Parker in his excitement.

"*What do you mean, what kind of protection will we have?*" cried Amy with curiosity in her voice.

"*As long as you are wearing the amulet, you will be protected from harm,*" replied Kadluk.

"*What do we need protection for? We don't have any enemies!*" stated Ty as he looked inquiringly at Kadluk.

"*Ty, mind your manners,*" Amy said giving him a stern look.

"Your enemies and things that will do you harm are not always known or visible to you which is why you must always be on your guard. The amulet will see that you are not taken by surprise and will forever be alert to any dangers that may befall you," Kadluk said.

"Well I haven't seen anything that we can't handle!" Ty informed the group in a boastful manner.

"Only time will tell what perils lie before you and what you can and cannot handle!" Kadluk sternly told the kids.

The kids knew without asking any questions that they were listening to the voice of experience. There was no need to question Kadluk. The tone of his voice said everything. They would have to be forever on guard for any trouble that may arise in the future. They took comfort in knowing the powers of the little amulet would provide them with protection as they explored the new world they found themselves in.

*   *   *

"What are you kids doing over by those dogs?" Nadine yelled from the kitchen with alarm in her voice.

"Nothing mom," replied Amy.

"Well get away from those dogs, your father said they're unpredictable. Come on, it's time for lunch," Nadine called to the kids.

"You're right Nadine, the kids shouldn't be near those dogs - they're dangerous. However, I don't think THE OLD ONE would let anything happen to them," Gwen advised Nadine.

"You're probably right but those dogs are just as wild as any wild animal, they're certainly not tame. It just scares me when I think about what could happen," Nadine replied with concern in her voice as she looked towards the kids.

"How old do you think THE OLD ONE is?" Gwen asked Nadine.

"I have no idea, I couldn't even hazard a guess," Nadine replied. She watched the kids start towards them before she turned with Gwen and entered the kitchen.

"We've got to go - when will we see you again?" Amy said as she turned to look at Kadluk. She had turned just in time to see Kadluk's dogs spring to life as he cracked his whip over their heads. Kadluk and his dog team quickly disappeared into the vast white wasteland of the barrens. Turning back to her brothers she said "I wish he hadn't left - I wanted to talk to him about the amulet some more. When he first looked at it I saw a fleeting look in his eyes, as

73

though he recognized it," Amy informed her brothers.

"Jiminy-Willie-Peppers, do you think Kadluk is the first shaman?" Parker howled.

"Don't be silly, that's not possible. No one could live that long!" scoffed Ty.

"Well, look what we've experienced so far! To us, none of this seems possible and yet it's happening," Amy cried.

"If you put it that way, I guess you're right. If it were not for the fact that I've been taking part in what has been occurring, I would never believe that all this could happen," Ty conceded.

"Amy, do you think Kadluk is the first shaman?" Parker blurted in excitement.

"I don't know, Parker, but I've got a feeling we'll never know if he doesn't want us to," Amy replied.

"From what I've seen, I'm beginning to think there's a lot we'll never know about THE OLD ONE," Ty murmured.

Amy and Parker nodded their heads in agreement as they reached the kitchen and went inside to join their mother and Gwen for lunch.

* * * THE END * * *

<u>GLOSSARY</u>

Inua – (inh' oo ah) n, the spiritual occupants, or spirit helpers, that reside in all living or inanimate things

Inuit – (in oo it) n, The People

Komatik (koh-ma-tik) n, a sled with wooden runners and crossbars bound with animal hides

Mukluk – n, an Inuit skin boot

Permafrost – n, ground that is permanently frozen

Shaman – (sham-man) n, 1. a priest of shamanism. 2. a medicine man or witch doctor of a similar religion. (they were thought to have special abilities in relating to the supernatural powers)

Shamanism – (sham-man-iz-zum) n, a religion of northern Asia, based on a belief in good and evil spirits who can be influenced or controlled only by the shamans. Shamanist n, adj.

Tarrak – n, a dark, angry, enraged and malicious spirit. If relatives did not adhere to certain taboos after a person's death, the dead person's soul became enraged and malicious. This dark angry spirit was known to some Inuit as a personal shade or tarrak.

The Author

Lawrence was born and raised in Alberta. 37 years of his adult life was spent serving in the Canadian Armed Forces and the Royal Canadian Mounted Police. The author draws on 10 years of living in the Yukon and the Northwest Territories for the inspiration for his stories. Retirement finds him again in Alberta where he presently lives with his wife Judith. They have 2 children and 6 grandchildren.

The Illustrator

Rob Adams, son of Lawrence Adams; when he is not working on his fathers illustrations, can be found working on game designs. Trained in Visual Communication, Rob currently works in the field of video games, juggling roles of a producer and game designer. Rob has had first hand experience of living and visiting many of the places described in the Trapps Family Adventure books.

Other books by Lawrence E.R. Adams.

The old one
The stolen soul

Watch for future books by Lawrence Adams as the Trapps Family Adventures continue to explore the mysteries of the north.

The creator
The stolen soul
The mine
The famine
who walks on my land
who swims in my waters
who flies in my skies
The spirit of marble island
The search for the red diamond
The little people
The rescue

Join Amy, Ty and Parker as they continue to seek answers to life's adventures on the frozen tundra.

GIVE A "**LAWRENCE E.R. ADAMS**" BOOK TO A FRIEND

Trapps Publishing
P.O. Box 212
Irricana, AB T0M 1B0
E-mail: trapps@efirehose.net
Send to:

Name:_____

Street:_____

City:_____

Province/

State:_____Zip Code_____

Please Send:

"THE OLD ONE"   ____ X @ $9.95 =_____

"THE AMULET"   ____ X @ $9.95 =_____

"THE STOLEN SOUL"   ____ X @ $9.95 =_____

Shipping and handling for first book @ $4.00
plus $1.00 each additional Book   =_____

5% GST =_____

Total amount enclosed: _____

Make cheque or money order payable to:
TRAPPS PUBLISHING
Price subject to change without prior notice.
ORDERS OUTSIDE OF CANADA must be paid in U.S. funds
by cheque or money order drawn on U.S. or Canadian Bank.
Sorry no C.O.D.'s.

Preaching the Easter Story